KT-219-883

Meet the Author and Illustrator
Peter Clover

What is your favourite animal?
I love cats
What is your favourite boy's name?
Bonehead
What is your favourite girl's name?
Jordan
What is your favourite food?
Roast potatoes and Yorkshire pudding
What is your favourite music?
American Soul and R&B
What is your favourite hobby?
Talking

To Stephen and Missy

Contents

BRIC-A-BRAC
ANTIQUES
1758

Chapter 1
Pretty Polly

Sammy Blue wanted a dog. He was desperate for one.

But he didn't want just any old, regular sized dog. Sammy wanted a whacking big Great Dane. Nothing else would do. Mum said he couldn't even have a titchy Yorkie. You see, they lived in a small flat above Mr Hackbone's bric-a-brac antique shop. It was a very small flat, in a very old house, which sat right on the edge of the harbour. Strong winds rattled the windows and sent sea spray full of salt and sand flying over the roof tiles.

"We can't possibly keep a dog up here in the flat!" said Mum. "We don't have a garden. Dogs need gardens. Dogs dig. It wouldn't be right. Anyway, Mr Hackbone wouldn't like it!"

"A cat, then!" begged Sammy. "How about a stonking big tomcat? Cats don't need gardens. Billions of people keep cats in flats. Cats love small spaces. They're famous for it – ask anyone!"

"Not a cat," said Dad, dropping his newspaper. "Never! Cats have sharp claws. Cats scratch. A cat up here would rip this place to pieces in ten seconds flat. How about a nice goldfish?"

"Boring," moaned Sammy. "And I'd get really dizzy watching it swim round and round all day. I'd probably start fainting every five minutes." He fell to the floor with his eyes rolling around in his head.

"A nice budgie, then?" chirped Mum, raising one eyebrow at Sammy.

"Not cool, budgies," groaned Sammy. "How about an ostrich? Or an eagle?"

In the end they settled for a parrot. A talking parrot with bright green feathers. Dad went out and bought it the following day.

Mr Hackbone didn't mind them having a parrot in the flat. He kindly gave Mum an old brass birdcage which he'd found years ago lying with all the rubbish in the cellar beneath the shop.

The cage was great. But the parrot was useless. It didn't say a word. Not a peep! Not a squawk! Zilch! Nothing!

"I thought this parrot was supposed to talk!" complained Sammy.

"Give Polly time," said Mum. "Let her get used to her surroundings. I expect she'll be talking her head off in a day or two." Mum pouted her lips and blew kisses through the bars of the brass cage.

Polly ruffled her feathers, then leaned back into space and fell off her perch. She swung upside down with her head resting in the seed tray.

"This bird's daft," said Sammy. "Flaming bonkers. Can't even sit on a perch properly. Some parrot!"

Polly dropped to the floor of her cage, scrabbled to her feet, gave a loud squawk and started to scratch around in all the grit and sawdust.

Sammy popped a grape through the bars and watched Polly kick it around like a football. Then she picked it up carefully with one clawed foot and peeled it with her curved beak. Polly liked grapes.

"Clever Polly," said Sammy. The parrot peered at him with beady black eyes. Then she did a poo!

"Pretty Polly. Pretty Polly," squawked Sammy. The parrot cocked her head to one side and waited for another grape.

After nine grapes, Sammy gave up. Apart from the odd nervous screech when she caught sight of herself in the mirror, Polly said nothing.

"Give her time," smiled Mum. "She's probably shy."

But three days passed and Polly didn't say a single word.

On the fourth day, which happened to be a Thursday, Sammy came clomping up the three flights of stairs and crashed into the small living room. He threw his school bag onto the settee and pulled off his sweatshirt.

"Pretty Birdie," said a voice from behind him. A squawky parrot voice, which came from the corner of the room where Polly's cage stood.

Sammy spun round. He couldn't believe it. At last, Polly had spoken. Or had she?

Sammy flung himself across the room and peered into the cage. Then he gave a sharp gasp of amazement. For there, sitting on the perch, was not just one bright green parrot, but two!

Chapter 2
A Feathered Phantom

"Wow!" Sammy was gobsmacked. At first he thought that Mum and Dad had surprised him with another parrot. But when he took a closer look, Sammy got quite a shock – along with a strange feeling which made all the small hairs on the back of his neck stand on end.

There was something very odd about this second parrot. Although it *seemed* to be there all right, it looked more like a hazy picture of a parrot than a real one. Its feathers were all fuzzy around the edges. There was something unreal and ghostly about it, as if it wasn't really there at all. And when Sammy stared at it closely, he could see right through it.

Polly sat entranced. She was gripping the wooden perch so tightly that her eyes bulged and nearly popped out. The second parrot snuggled up close and ruffled its feathers as it cooed and repeated her name over and over again.

"Polly, Polly. Pretty Polly. Pretty Polly."

Sammy's parrot was nervous and timid. This new one was bold and brassy – very confident and a bit of a show-off, in fact.

"Pretty Polly. Who's a pretty Polly, then? Phwoaarrhhh!" The new parrot squawked again and again. Really loudly.

Sammy's mouth dropped open but no sound came out. He wanted to speak, to say something … anything. But, before he could gather his thoughts, the phantom parrot vanished. Like a wisp of candle smoke it dissolved into thin air, right before his very eyes. Threads of silver floated and twisted upwards through the bars of the cage. Then, poof! The phantom parrot was gone.

Sammy didn't say a word to anyone. But that night he couldn't sleep. Not a wink. He kept getting up, tiptoeing into the living room and checking on Polly.

"Check it out! Check it out!" said Sammy to himself.

Had he imagined it? Had he really seen a second parrot? A phantom with feathers? Perhaps he was dreaming! At last, worn out, Sammy fell into a deep sleep. And as the first light of morning sneaked in through a chink in his bedroom curtains, Mum yelled from the kitchen: "BREAKFAST!"

Sammy leaped out of bed and raced into the living room. Polly was in her cage. And so was the phantom parrot. He was sitting really close to Polly and leaning up against her so that her feathers were all squashed and sticking out through the bars.

Sammy rubbed his eyes in case he was dreaming. No – the phantom parrot was still there. This was cool. Dead cool! "Where did you come from?" whispered Sammy quietly, so that Mum wouldn't hear.

"Captain Crabmeat's a clever boy," squawked the parrot, eyeing Polly. "Polly, Polly. Pretty Polly. Cor, give us a kiss, me darling!" This parrot could really talk. It was brilliant!

Suddenly, Mum called again from the kitchen. And as Sammy spun round he

caught sight of a monster cat. A whacking big red tom. It lay, curled up on the armchair, snuggled down on Sammy's sweatshirt.

"A CAT!" Sammy couldn't believe it. He shivered as he suddenly noticed its fuzzy red fur. Like the phantom parrot, the outline of this cat was hazy. It shimmered like the ghostly image of a cat that wasn't really there at all. But it *was* there! Sammy could see it as plain as day.

"Sammy!" Mum called again. "Breakfast! Now!"

With a parting glance at the cat, Sammy dragged himself off to the kitchen.

No sooner had he sat down at the breakfast table than the cat followed him through. It launched itself into the air and landed on his lap, where it settled. It weighed a ton. Sammy felt the warm body against his knees. Sharp claws gripped his flesh. Sammy stroked the cat and felt its soft red fur beneath his hand.

Mum and Dad said nothing. It was quite clear that they couldn't see the cat. Just like the parrot, it could only be seen by Sammy.

"Shiver me timbers. Polly, Polly. Pretty, pretty, Polly," Captain Crabmeat was squawking in the next room at the top of his voice, but Mum and Dad didn't stir, or move a single muscle. They couldn't hear a thing!

Sammy shovelled down his breakfast and got ready for school. He left the red cat curled up asleep on his bed. Leaving the house that morning was one of the most difficult things he'd ever had to do in his entire life. Sammy wanted to stick around and find out exactly what was going on. Number one, he wanted to see if the cat would disappear again, like the parrot. And number two, he wanted to see if anything else was going to appear out of thin air.

Chapter 3
An Unexpected Visitor

The school day really dragged. It was Friday and they were breaking up early for half term. Workmen were coming in to shift all the desks so the classroom floors could be varnished. Everyone was being sent home at three o'clock.

Sammy raced all the way home. He ran up the stairs to the flat three at a time and let himself in with his key.

Mum worked part-time downstairs in Mr Hackbone's bric-a-brac antique shop. She wouldn't be coming up to the flat until at least half-past three. That meant that Sammy had half an hour all to himself.

First things first. Sammy dashed into the living room. Polly and Crabmeat were kissing and cuddling in the corner of the parrot cage. Polly seemed to be enjoying the company and attention of her phantom admirer.

"Polly, Polly. Pretty Polly," squawked Crabmeat as Sammy entered the room. "Splice the mainbrace. Weigh the anchor. Pieces of eight. Pieces of eight."

Once Crabmeat started to talk he just wouldn't shut up. He seemed to be really excited about something.

All at once, Sammy felt a strange fizzing in the air.

He looked around for the red cat. But the big tom wasn't in the living room. In fact, the cat was nowhere to be seen. Sammy had left his bedroom door open a crack in case the big cat wanted to stretch his legs. But that seemed a stupid idea now. After all, if the cat could appear out of thin air, then it could probably pass through walls and doors anytime it wanted. Sammy checked his room. Nothing there!

Maybe it's in the kitchen? thought Sammy. But no. He checked out the entire flat, which didn't take long, then gave up and went back to his room again. This time, as he pushed open the door and stepped inside, Sammy gasped. The sight before him took his breath away.

There, lying on his bed, was not just *one* cat, but two. Two whacking great brutes, one red and one striped, curled up together on the duvet. And there was more … much more. Sitting in a chair, flicking through Sammy's footie magazines was a young lad.

Sammy's mouth fell open. The boy dropped the magazines and stared back at Sammy from across the room.

He was about the same age as Sammy, but pale grey in colour from head to toe. And Sammy could see right through him. He was dressed in shabby trousers, cut off at the knee, and a tatty cotton shirt. His hair was long, matted and tied back at the neck in a rat's tail. There was also a definite smell of salt and seaweed coming from *his* corner of the room.

Sammy looked down at the boy's bare feet. They were black and grubby and seemed to blend into the thick pile of the carpet.

The boy spoke first.

"Ahoy, shipmate!" He sounded bright and cheerful. Not at all shocked or surprised, as Sammy was. "My name's Smitty. Welcome aboard," he added, with a cheeky grin.

Sammy was stunned. "Hi," was all he could manage to say.

"Strike up the Jolly Roger," screeched Crabmeat from the living room. "Pieces of eight. Pieces of eight."

The boy roared with laughter and Sammy found himself laughing too! The crazy parrot seemed to have broken the spell.

And Sammy found his voice.

"Where the flipping heck did you come from?" he squeaked, sounding like a balloon with all the air escaping. "And what are you doing here ... in my room?" Sammy didn't mean to sound so rude. But it just sort of came out that way. Sammy thought he must have sounded like an angry mouse. He hoped the boy didn't notice. After all, it was quite a shock for him to find a ghost sitting in his room.

Sadly, Smitty *did* notice and suddenly looked very upset. The bright cheerful spark inside him faded and died. It was almost as if Sammy had switched him off like a lamp. His light had gone out.

"Sorry!" said the boy, faintly. "I didn't think you'd mind if I dropped in." Then he slowly closed his eyes and faded into thin air, leaving only the faint smell of the sea behind him.

"Come back!" called Sammy. "It's all right. Come back! You can stay. I *want* you to stay." But the boy didn't return. He had gone.

Sammy spun around to face the bed. The two cats had gone too! He flew into the living room. Polly sat alone on her perch. She looked confused and upset with her feathers all ruffled.

"Pretty Polly. Pretty Polly." It was the first time that Polly had ever spoken. But it was a sound filled with sadness. Crabmeat had gone too!

Chapter 4
Shiver me Timbers

Mum came up from the shop at exactly 3.30 and straight away sent Sammy out to buy bread and milk at Supa Shopper. Sammy dragged his feet. He couldn't stop thinking about Smitty and all the other strange things which had happened in the past few days.

Sammy wished that he'd been more friendly to the ghost who had appeared in his room. And he wondered if the boy would ever come back. It wasn't an impossible idea. After all, Crabmeat had already turned up twice!

Sammy still didn't tell his parents about the "phantom visits". They would probably never have believed him anyway, simply because *they* couldn't see anything. And everyone knows that ghosts aren't real!

On the way back from Supa Shopper, Sammy stopped outside in the street and looked up at the windows of the flat. He stood on the cobbled pavement with the harbour behind him and studied the whole front of the building. Sammy was suddenly seeing it for the first time. Really seeing it. Seeing it in a new light for exactly what it was – a very old building.

Although Sammy didn't know how old the building was, he sensed that it was very old indeed. The shop front of Mr Hackbone's bric-a-brac antique shop had crooked bay windows with tiny glass panes. And above the door were numbers carved into the stone lintel. Sammy couldn't quite make out what the numbers were, but it looked like a date: 1758. Wow! This building was much older than he thought!

Sammy had never noticed the carved lintel before. He was curious and decided to ask Mr Hackbone about it in the morning. But before morning came, something much more strange and curious happened!

That night, as Sammy sat up in bed reading his footie mags before he went to sleep, his nose started twitching. Sammy suddenly became aware of a fishy, seaweed-like smell in the room.

He took a long, deep sniff. And when he looked up, he gasped. There, at the foot of his bed, was the ghostly form of the boy. Sammy's eyes grew wide as thin trails of silver smoke twisted themselves into the shape of Smitty.

Sammy was startled, but pleased at the same time. The two big cats had returned as well and were padding around on his bed, treading the duvet before they plonked themselves down on his soft pillows.

Then he heard Crabmeat squawking his beak off next door.

"Hello!" whispered Sammy to Smitty. This time he was extra careful to make his voice sound friendly. "I'm sorry about last time you were here. I'm glad you've come back!"

Sammy wanted to talk and find out what was behind these strange visits.

"I hope you don't mind," smiled Smitty. His eyes twinkled like diamonds. "But I've brought a few more friends along with me."

Sammy wondered what he meant by *a few more friends!* But even before he had time to ask, eleven members of the good ship the *Black Crow* stepped through the stone walls into his bedroom.

The strong smell of herring and the sea was overpowering. Sammy could hear the creaks and groans of the old ship's timbers in his ears, as he stared hard at the assembled pirate crew. For that's what they were ... *PIRATES*.

There was Bacon, the ship's cook, Doc Bones and Squire Delaney. There was Boris the Bosun, and seven sulky deck hands, all dressed in funny clothes with cut off trews and flashy waistcoats. The ragged bunch looked like film extras from *Treasure Island*! The sight of them all sucked Sammy's breath away. He could hardly breathe. He was so excited. Sammy bubbled like lemonade.

MUM

Chapter 5
Red Beard the Really Rotten

Sammy sat bolt upright in bed and gawped, speechless and goggle eyed, at the amazing sight before him.

"Is it all right if we stay?" asked Smitty. "We won't get in the way. We won't take up any space and no one can see us except you and your parrot!"

Somehow, that was supposed to make everything OK. *But what if Mum finds out*?

thought Sammy. *She'd go ballistic. She'd hit the roof. She'd probably call* Ghostbusters *or something!*

But it was almost bedtime, so Sammy didn't think it would hurt if they stayed for maybe one night. He didn't in fact say that! He just nodded his head at them. Suddenly, a hearty chorus of "Yo ho ho and a bottle of rum" burst out from the pirate crew. Sammy pushed his fingers into his ears. Surely Mum and Dad could hear that! They were only in the next room watching TV. Sammy expected them to come bursting into his bedroom. But they didn't.

As far as ghosts are concerned, Mum and Dad must be blind and stone deaf, he thought.

At last, the crew calmed down, and somehow settled themselves like sardines into Sammy's bed, with the covers pulled up to their whiskery chins. The amazing thing was that they didn't take up much space at all. The air tingled with electric excitement. Then the talking and the explaining began. Sammy told them all about school. But he had so many questions of his own to ask. Who were they all? Where did they come from? What did they want?

This is what Sammy learnt:

Two hundred and fifty years ago, in a time of sailing ships and pirate galleons, Smitty and his friends were cabin boy and crew aboard the *Black Crow*, a pirate ship that roamed the Seven Seas.

Crabmeat was the *Black Crow*'s lucky mascot. And the two big cats were master rat catchers. For years the *Black Crow* sailed the trade routes, robbing and plundering. But the crew didn't want to be outlaws. They wanted to be regular jolly

sailors. They had been forced into a pirate life by the evil Red Beard the Really Rotten.

The crew were clearly scared stiff of this Red Beard the Really Rotten. They told Sammy how one day they had planned a mutiny against him. They got Red Beard the Really Rotten blind drunk on Jamaican rum, then forced him to walk the plank.

But almost straight away tragedy had struck. The ship hit a big rock and the *Black Crow* sank. Everyone on board was drowned. But that wasn't the end of it. There was much worse to come. The crew became wandering ghosts, and since then had been roaming the endless oceans of lost souls. They were unable to rest for fear of being caught by Red Beard. He had been chasing them, nonstop, for two hundred and fifty years, seeking revenge.

"Wow!" Sammy could hardly believe what he was hearing. "But why have you come here?" he asked, nervously. Sammy was starting to get a little worried. "Won't this Red Beard the Really Rotten be able to follow you and come here too?" he asked.

The crew looked shifty and exchanged worried glances.

Smitty spoke. "It was Crabmeat who found the way through the mist. He was pulled here from the other side. This place seemed safe enough. Once the parrot had passed safely through onto your side we sent the cats. Then I came."

"But we're still not sure how safe it is," added the Squire. "We've never found a hiding place like this before! And we're so tired. We can't keep running for ever. We just need a rest."

Sammy wondered if Polly or the brass birdcage had anything to do with all this. After all, the cage *was* very old. And Mr Hackbone *had* told Mum that it had been hanging around in the cellar for years. In fact, it might have been hanging around since 1758.

No one seemed to know where the cage first came from. But Sammy didn't think it mattered any more. The pirate crew were what mattered now! They were right there tucked up in his bed. And who knew what would happen next!

Chapter 6
A Storm is Brewing

After hours and hours of wild pirate storytelling, at last Sammy fell fast asleep. He was quite pleased to find his bedroom empty when he woke up the next morning. Sammy felt worn out.

The welcoming smell of grilled bacon floated through the flat from the kitchen. Sammy rubbed his eyes. Perhaps last night had been nothing but a fantastic dream after all! He decided to pop down to see Mr Hackbone first thing after breakfast, and ask about the building *and* the parrot cage. For some strange reason, Sammy was certain that the two things were somehow linked.

He pulled on his tracksuit bottoms over his pyjamas, and slipped on a sweatshirt. Then he padded barefoot into the kitchen.

The first thing that Sammy saw was Smitty, sitting in *his* place at the table, with Crabmeat perched on his shoulder.

Then he felt something soft and furry against his feet. Glancing down, Sammy saw the two monster cats rubbing themselves against his legs.

"Morning, Sam," chirped Mum. "Breakfast is ready." She flipped two eggs and rashers of crispy bacon onto a plate.

Smitty licked his lips. He hadn't eaten in years. Two hundred and fifty years to be exact. And he'd *never* seen bacon like this!

Sammy gave Smitty a sideways nod and signalled with his eyes for him to move into the next chair. Then Sammy sat down.

Dad came in with his newspaper and plonked himself down in a chair on the other side of the table. Then, without any warning, the entire crew of the *Black Crow* stepped through the plaster wall behind him, and stood, looming over the table, drooling at Sammy's plate of bacon and eggs.

"Shiver me timbers. Splice the mainbrace! Pieces of eight! Pieces of eight!" Crabmeat landed on Sammy's shoulder and squawked loudly in his ear. Sammy winced, but Dad didn't even notice and carried on reading his newspaper. Mum poured the tea.

"It's a bit warm in here this morning," she said. "No air." Then Mum flung open the window and glanced across the harbour and up at the sky. "Judging by the colour of those clouds over the sea, I'd say there was a big storm coming," she added. "Goodness, it's close in here. I can hardly breathe."

Nor can I, thought Sammy. He didn't say anything. He just sat there and his face turned pale. The air in the flat did feel a bit thick. In fact it felt so thick, you could almost cut it with a knife. Or a cutlass. The very air was beginning to feel ... crowded.

Sammy couldn't touch his breakfast. He sensed that Smitty and his pirate friends had something to do with this cramped feeling and the looming storm. He stared past his dad at Smitty, who now stood waiting behind him with his mouth dribbling at the sight of the loaded plate of food.

"This bacon smells a bit funny," remarked Dad. "A bit like ... seaweed!" He lifted a whole rasher on his fork and took a deep sniff. The smell of the ocean filled the small kitchen. Then the bacon vanished. And Smitty stood, licking his lips. Crabmeat squawked and Dad just stared at his empty fork.

Outside, the sky grew even darker and the crew suddenly became worried and restless. They exchanged quick glances and Doc Bones muttered something under his breath. The room buzzed with static electricity. The storm was right above the house.

Sammy felt a strange tingling across his scalp as all the hair on his head stood on end. Then a deep rumble behind the black clouds shook the windows and a flash of lightning lit up the room with a brilliant white light.

Mum screamed. Crabmeat fainted and fell off Sammy's shoulder. And Red Beard the Really Rotten appeared at the open kitchen doorway seething with rage.

He wore a heavy grey coat and a three-cornered pirate hat. He had one wooden leg and a metal hook in place of a hand. He also wore a patch over one eye. It seemed to Sammy that there was quite a lot of him missing. But what was left was more than enough to scare the wits out of him.

Two hundred and fifty years of anger and fury oozed from his every pore. Smoke poured from his nostrils and red flames sparked and crackled from his big, bushy beard. The ghost of Red Beard the Really Rotten pulled himself up to his full height. He was six foot tall and as wide as a barn door. The sight was terrifying. The air popped and fizzed with his presence.

Then Red Beard began to grin, a salty fierce grin that flashed all over his ugly face, like lightning across the battered sky outside.

The crew gasped. And Smitty's eyes grew as big as the breakfast plates.

Red Beard glared at his long-lost crew. "At last!" he bellowed. His breath smelled of stale kippers. "At last! Revenge is mine!"

Chapter 7
The Final Revenge

Mum slammed the kitchen window shut and bolted it.

"What's that horrible smell?" she said, looking at Dad and crinkling her nose. Red Beard roared again, pulling a flintlock pistol from his belt.

Sammy ducked under the table and sent his breakfast flying across the room.

"Sammy, what on earth are you doing?" exclaimed Mum. "It's only an electric storm!"

Thunder exploded overhead as Red Beard fired his pistol. The first shot whistled past Dad's ear and shattered the teapot. Mum screamed as Smitty and the entire crew crashed past her and tried to hide inside the fridge.

The lightning flashed again and Dad jumped to his feet. He had never known a thunderstorm to smash crockery before. Red Beard fired another pistol shot and a teacup exploded. Sammy peered out from under the table. It was all too much.

Then something even more amazing happened ... A woman appeared ... out of nowhere. She was short and dumpy. She wore a cotton mop cap and a long apron that swept the floor. Her face was ruddy and plump and she waved a soup ladle in her fist, like a warrior's club.

"Robert Red Beard," she bellowed, in a voice that could probably sink ships, "where in the King's name have you been? You ran off and left me with a brood of brats to feed and a house that was falling to bits. You've a lot of explaining to do, husband!"

The fridge door creaked open and Smitty stuck his head out, just in time to see Mrs Red Beard take a swipe at her husband with the enormous soup ladle. The giant pirate ran for his life as the little woman chased him out of the kitchen. "Running off to sea and leaving me with a lifetime of struggle and strife," she bellowed after him. "You'll not get away from me this time, you skulking, fish-faced sea dog. I'll have your guts for garters and your ears for mug handles."

Red Beard the Really Rotten didn't hang around for a second longer. Suddenly he forgot all about revenge. In a flash he had stumped down the hall at a hundred miles an hour, and was gone for ever, with Mrs Red Beard hot on his trail. He left nothing behind but a trail of smoking ash and the smell of rotten fish.

Outside, the storm passed and the sun came out. Sammy somehow knew that Smitty and the crew would never be bothered by Red Beard again. One by one they came out of hiding and sneaked out of the room.

Mum and Dad were busy clearing away the mess on the table and floor with a dustpan and brush.

"Phew! I've never known a storm like it," they were saying. This gave Sammy the chance he needed to slip away to his bedroom.

Smitty was standing there with the crew, and they were laughing their heads off.

"Fancy old Red Beard being chased off like that by his own lady wife."

"She did look mean, though, didn't she?" grinned the Squire. "He'll spend the rest of his wretched days keeping out of *her* way, that's for sure."

The sun streamed brightly in through Sammy's bedroom window as one by one the crew said goodbye and faded back into the grey mist from where they had come.

"Come on, lads. We've got to find a ship," said Boris the Bosun. Some passed through the walls. Some floated up through the ceiling. And some simply faded into the pattern on the carpet.

Crabmeat was the last to go. With one final squawk and one final nuzzle with Polly, he pecked her on the head and vanished.

Sammy felt terribly sad. It had been really exciting having Smitty and his pirate pals around. And now they had all gone.

Polly looked sad too. She puffed out her feathers and squeezed her eyes tight shut. She seemed to be missing Crabmeat as much as Sammy was missing Smitty. Sammy decided to give himself something to do by cleaning and polishing Polly's cage.

As Sammy set to with Brillo pads and Brasso, he suddenly saw a nameplate which he hadn't noticed before on its base. It was a small metal plate like the ones on football trophies. At first there didn't seem to be anything written on it. But, as Sammy rubbed and polished, the name *Captain Crabmeat* shone through, bright and clear.

Sammy smiled to himself. Now it all made sense. He didn't have to ask Mr Hackbone after all. It was Crabmeat's cage which had brought them all through from the other side. And it was Polly who had given the cage a new life.

Sammy carried the cage through into his bedroom. He'd decided that he wanted Polly to live in his room from now on. She reminded him of the pirates.

"Ahoy there, shipmate!"

Sammy nearly dropped the cage when he heard it. He spun round. It was Smitty and the crew. Or at least their heads, poking through Sammy's bedroom wall.

"We decided not to go after all," they grinned. "We thought it might be more fun

to hang out here for a while. That is, if there's room on board?"

Sammy laughed. "How much room exactly does a phantom pirate crew take up?" he asked.

"As much space as mischief allows," grinned Smitty. "Now tell us all about this place called school again."

Sammy hugged himself and felt all tingly inside. He wasn't going to tell anyone about this. Smitty and the crew were going to be his own special secret. His own special friends. But he was definitely going to take them to school. That idea seemed really cool. Dead Cool! And Sammy couldn't wait!

Barrington Stoke would like to thank all its readers for commenting on the manuscript before publication and in particular:

Toby Ackland
Wendy Atkinson
Charlie Baker
Victoria Bull
Hannah Cann
Naomi Clarke
Peter Dodd
Annie Foreman
Jennifer Gibney
Kiran Gill
Stephanie Hanlon
Charlotte Jones
Moira Kleissner
Kara Lekuse
Ian McCarthy
Jake Sanders
Mrs P. Smith
Stephanie Stoneham
Nathan Vinton
Phillipa Wright

Become a Consultant!

Would you like to give us feedback on our titles before they are published? Contact us at the address or website below – we'd love to hear from you!

Barrington Stoke, 10 Belford Terrace, Edinburgh EH4 3DQ
Tel: 0131 315 4933 Fax: 0131 315 4934
E-mail: info@barringtonstoke.co.uk
Website: www.barringtonstoke.co.uk